For my sisters and brothers:
Beth, Mary, Michael,
Tim, and Gerry

CHAPTER ONE

Laura Lee watched Mom and Dad
paint the kitchen.

Mom stirred the paint.

Dad climbed a tall ladder.

"Can I help?" asked Laura Lee.

"Maybe later," said Mom.

LEARN TO READ

A Victory for LAURA LEE

Library
Clifton Park
Baptist Church

by Alice Sullivan Finlay
illustrated by Julie Durrell

ZondervanPublishingHouse
Grand Rapids, Michigan

A Division of HarperCollinsPublishers

$$\begin{array}{c} e \ ^{\supset} \\ F \ 1 \ N \end{array}$$

A Victory for Laura Lee
Text copyright © 1993 by Alice Sullivan Finlay
Illustration copyright © 1993 by Julie Durrell

Requests for information should be addressed to:
Zondervan Publishing House
Grand Rapids, Michigan 49530

Library of Congress Cataloging-in-Publication Data

Finlay, Alice Sullivan.
   A victory for Laura Lee / Alice Sullivan Finlay.
     p. cm.
   Summary: After rescuing an injured duck, Laura Lee tries to clean
up a polluted pond.
   ISBN 0-310-59851-6 (pbk.)
   [1. Wildlife rescue—Fiction. 2. Environmental protection—
Fiction. 3. Pollution—Fiction. 4. Ponds—Fiction.] I. Title.
PZ7.F49579Vi   1993
[E]–dc20   93-3501
                                         CIP
                                         AC

Edited by Dave Lambert and Leslie Kimmelman
Interior and cover design by Steven M. Scott
Illustrations by Julie Durrell

Printed in the United States of America

93 94 95 96 97 98 / CH / 10 9 8 7 6 5 4 3 2 1

"I want to climb the ladder,"
said Randy.

He started to climb.

Mom pulled him down.

"Why don't you two
go feed the ducks," said Mom.

"Will you come with us?"
asked Laura Lee.

"Not today," said Mom.

Laura Lee frowned.

She grabbed the bag of old bread.

Laura Lee's family always fed
the ducks together.

Now Mom and Dad were too busy.

Laura Lee walked toward the pond.

Randy ran after her.

The girl from next door
waved to them.

"Hi, Deni," called Laura Lee.

"Want to go to the pond?"

"Sure," said Deni.

Deni walked with
Laura Lee and Randy.

They walked to the pond.
The lily pads bloomed
with big, yellow flowers.
Laura Lee wished Mom and Dad
could see the flowers, too.
"This is the best day ever,"
said Randy.
"It could be," said Laura Lee.

CHAPTER TWO

The pond was pretty.

A big weeping willow tree

drooped over the pond.

Ducks paddled along the shore.

"Quack, quack, quack,"

the ducks said.

"These ducks are beautiful,"

said Laura Lee.

"Yes," said Randy.

"But I like frogs better."

They listened to the frogs.

They listened to the crickets.

They walked around the pond

to the ducks.

"Quack, quack, quack."
The ducks were waiting for food.
Laura Lee shared the bread
with Deni and Randy.
"Quack, quack."
Some of the ducks had
pretty green heads.

The ducks swam
toward the children,
leaving *V*'s in the water
behind them.
They gobbled up the bread.
Laura Lee threw bread
to the ducks on the ground.
They waddled toward the bread.
They wiggled their tails
back and forth.
"Quack, quack, quack."
Laura Lee loved to feed the ducks.
When the bread was gone,
Randy raced along the shore.

"I'm going to catch a frog," he said.

"Yuck," said Deni.

"I don't like to touch them."

"I see one jumping," said Randy.

He ran to the water's edge.

He put his hands in the mud.

But the frog darted away.

"He's slippery!" cried Randy.

Laura Lee laughed.

"I'm glad he got away," said Deni.

"Look over there," said Randy.

"I think a duck is stuck

under a lily pad."

"Where?" asked Laura Lee.

Randy pointed.

"We have to help him," said Deni.

Laura Lee took off her shoes.

The mud squished between her toes.

She waded to the lily pads.

"He has plastic around his neck,"

she said. "Come and help me."

Deni and Randy waded
into the pond.
They grabbed the duck.
"This plastic is choking him!"
cried Laura Lee.
She pulled one end of the plastic
loose from the lily pad.
The other end stuck tight
around the duck's neck.
Laura Lee carried the duck
to the shore.
"Randy, run and get a box,"
she said.
The duck was too weak to fight.
"Why do people have to throw
their trash in the pond?"
asked Laura Lee.

Laura Lee and Deni walked
toward home.

Randy ran to them with a box.

Laura Lee put the duck into the box.

"Can we save his life?"
asked Randy.

"It could be," said Laura Lee.

CHAPTER THREE

Laura Lee carried the box carefully.

"Go tell Dad we need him,"

she told Randy.

The duck was hardly breathing.

Laura Lee's heart pounded.

She hoped they could save the duck.

Dad came running.

He looked at the duck.

"Let's get that plastic off," he said.

"Then he will have a chance."

Dad carried the box
into the playroom.

"We need scissors," he called.

Mom gave him a pair of scissors.

Laura Lee's heart thumped harder.

"I hope he makes it," said Deni.

"Me, too," said Laura Lee.

She held her breath.

Dad carefully cut the plastic.

He took it from the duck's neck.

"There," said Dad.

Laura Lee let out a long breath.

"Should we take him to a vet?"

she asked.

"We will if he is not better

by tomorrow," Dad replied.

"I hope we saved him," said Deni.

Laura Lee held her friend's hand.

She was glad Deni cared

about the duck, too.

They put bread and water
into the box.

"I think the duck
is breathing better," said Dad.

Laura Lee smiled.

"I'm ordering pizza," said Mom.

"Deni, can you stay for dinner?"

Deni called her mother.

"It's all right," Deni said.

Randy sat by the duck's box.

Laura Lee and Deni
went into the kitchen.

"Why do people litter?"
asked Laura Lee.

"I wish I knew," said Mom.

Dad sat at the table.

He picked up his Bible and read,

" 'Be doers of the word,

and not hearers only.' James 1:22."

He closed his Bible.

"We will do something about the pond

when we finish painting," said Dad.

"But that could be days,"

said Laura Lee.

Laura Lee and Deni
looked at each other.
"If we wait, more ducks
could be hurt," said Laura Lee.
"Can we do something
by ourselves?" whispered Deni.
"It could be," said Laura Lee.

CHAPTER FOUR

In the morning, Laura Lee
and Randy ran to the playroom.
"He's alive!" cried Laura Lee.
"All right!" said Randy.
The duck looked at them.
He moved his neck.
He drank some water.
Mom and Dad came
from the kitchen.

Randy tried to pet the duck.

The duck pecked Randy's hand.

"Don't touch him," warned Mom.

"I want him to be my pet,"
said Randy.

Dad shook his head.

"This duck is wild.

He belongs outdoors.

That is his home."

Laura Lee looked out the window
at the pond.

"The pond is his home," she said.
"But it is full of trash.
We have to do something about it."

"We will finish painting
in a few days," said Dad.
"Then we will do something."

Laura Lee ate a bowl of cereal.
She watched the duck.

Laura Lee was glad the duck
was alive.
But she was also angry.
The duck could have died
because someone was careless.

I have to do something,
she thought.

Laura Lee remembered
the Bible verse Dad had read.
She wanted to be a doer—
right now!
She went to get Deni.
"Let's round up all the kids,"
Laura Lee said.
"We will clean up the pond
by ourselves."
"Good idea," agreed Deni.

Laura Lee and Deni went to
every house on the block.
Kids of all ages came to the pond.
They stood waiting to be told
what to do.
Laura Lee was nervous.
How could she be in charge of
so many kids?
She swallowed hard.
Then she told them about the duck.
"The duck almost died," she said.
"Please, all of you—
help us clean up the pond.
Help keep the animals safe."

The kids started working.

They picked up cans and paper.

They picked up plastic.

They put everything
in garbage bags.

"This looks great," said Randy.

Laura Lee smiled.

She thanked everyone for helping.

"Let's try to keep it this way,"
she told them.

The pond was clean.

"Quack, quack, quack."

Even the ducks seemed pleased.

"This pond is even better now,"
said Deni.

"It could be," said Laura Lee.

CHAPTER FIVE

The next morning,

Laura Lee checked the duck.

"He looks better," said Randy.

The duck drank water and ate corn.

He spread his wings.

"He's trying to fly," said Randy.

"Can we take him to the pond?"

"Wait until he's stronger,"

said Dad.

Laura Lee hummed a happy tune.

When the duck was stronger,

he would have a clean home to go to.

"Let's go look at the pond,"

she said.

"Tag, you're it!" cried Randy.

They raced to the pond.

When they got there,

Laura Lee and Randy

both stopped quickly.

Someone had dumped garbage

near the water.

The pond smelled like rotten food.

Laura Lee made a fist.

"Who did this?" she asked loudly.

Laura Lee and Randy rounded up
the kids again.

This time, even more came.

"Another cleanup?" a boy asked.

"Something else, too," said Laura Lee.

Everyone bagged the garbage.

Then Laura Lee brought out
markers and cardboard.

"We will march around the pond,"
said Laura Lee.

"When the grown-ups see us,
maybe they will finally do something."

The children made signs.

They spread out around the pond.

They marched back and forth.

"Save the pond!
Save the ducks!" they shouted.

Parents and neighbors heard the
noise and came out to see.
Some of them
marched with the children.
One neighbor scowled at them.

"Stop this racket
or I will call the police," he said.
Laura Lee was frightened.
Then Mom and Dad
joined in the march, too.
"Keep going," Laura Lee told
her friends.
A police car drove up.
Will they take me away?
Laura Lee wondered.
The policeman talked
to the grouchy neighbor.
"Make them stop," said the man.
"I can't," said the policeman.
"They are marching peacefully."
"I'm calling the mayor,"
said the angry man.

Dad looked at Laura Lee.

"Did you start this?" he asked.

She nodded.

"We are proud of you," said Mom.

"We're sorry we were too busy to help."

"But we're not too busy any more,"

said Dad. "This park could be

a nice place for ducks and for people."

"It could be," said Laura Lee.

CHAPTER SIX

In the evening, the phone rang.

When Dad hung up, he said,

"That was the mayor.

They will put up signs

against littering.

Volunteers will help keep
the pond clean."

"All right!" cheered Randy.

"This is your victory,
Laura Lee," said Mom.

Laura Lee shook her head.

"Not until the duck goes home."

She turned the box on its side.

The duck shook his wings.

He waddled across the floor.

Dad nodded.

"He's strong enough now," he said.

They took the duck to the pond.

A red sunset blazed across the sky.

Laura Lee liked the way God
said good night.

She set the duck near the water.

He waddled and shook his tail.

"Now you're home," said Laura Lee.

"Quack, quack, quack."

The duck answered the other ducks.

He walked into the water.

He paddled away

and joined his friends.

Laura Lee felt a little sad

but also happy.

The family watched the sky
turn from red to purple.
They listened to
the bullfrogs and crickets.
"Quack, quack, quack."
"The ducks are happy," said Dad.
"Laura Lee, you are a doer."
Laura Lee's heart
filled with happiness.
"What will you tackle next?"
asked Mom.
"Cleaning up the whole country?"
Laura Lee grinned.
"It could be," said Laura Lee.

The End

Did you enjoy this book about Laura Lee? I have good news—there are *more* Laura Lee books! Read about them on the following pages.

The Laura Lee books are available at your local Christian bookstore, or you can order direct from 800-727-3480.

Don't miss...

Zondervan Publishing House
0-310-59841-9

Laura Lee and the Monster Sea

**There's a monster in the sea...
and Laura Lee wants to go home.**

Laura Lee and her family are on vacation at the seashore. But Laura Lee is afraid. The waves roar like a monster. Seaweed grabs her feet. Her brother, Randy, chases her with a clam.

With the help of her family, can Laura Lee learn not to be frightened?

Don't miss...

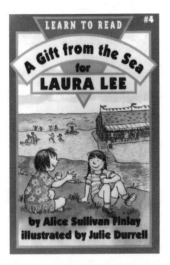

Zondervan Publishing House
0-310-59871-0

A Gift from the Sea for Laura Lee

**Laura Lee's friend Shona is rich...
but Laura Lee is not.**

When Laura Lee and her family visit her grandma at the seashore, Laura Lee meets Shona. But Shona says that her family is rich. Will Shona still like Laura Lee even though Laura Lee's family is not rich? Will Laura Lee tell Shona the truth? And who will win the fishing contest?

Laura Lee's dad and grandma help her solve a tough problem in *A Gift from the Sea for Laura Lee*.

Don't miss...

Zondervan Publishing House
0-310-59861-3

Laura Lee and the Little Pine Tree

A cabin without lights, water... or a bathroom?

That's where Laura Lee and her family are spending the week, high in the mountains. Having to pump their own water and use an old outhouse for a bathroom is bad enough. But who is stealing their food? Is it a bear? And why did it have to snow? And what can Laura Lee do when her brother Randy disappears?

"This is too much for me," says Laura Lee.

Date Due